# SNOW IN THE GARDEN
## A FIRST BOOK OF CHRISTMAS

Shirley Hughes

WALKER BOOKS
AND SUBSIDIARIES

LONDON · BOSTON · SYDNEY · AUCKLAND

# A Note from Shirley Hughes

Winter is a wonderfully evocative time for
inspiring artwork, I find; the pattern of bare branches
against a pale sky, snow and frost on the ground
throwing every twig and branch into sharp detail,
and the extra warmth it gives to figures set in
this kind of landscape. It is thrilling to see
my winter stories and poems, alternating with
seasonal recipes and things to do and make,
in this beautifully produced collection.

*Shirley Hughes*

# CONTENTS

# Cold

Cold fingers,
Cold toes,
Pink sky,
Pink nose.
Hard ground,
Bare trees,
Branches crack,
Puddles freeze.
Frost white,
Sun red,
Warm room,
Warm bed.

# Red Robin Decorations

*You can make these colourful decorations to hang on a Christmas tree, or even use them as gift labels for presents!*

## You will need:
A4 sheet of red paper
A4 sheet of brown card
Stick-on eyes
A glue stick
A pencil (or crayon)
A hole punch
Red ribbon (or string)
Scissors

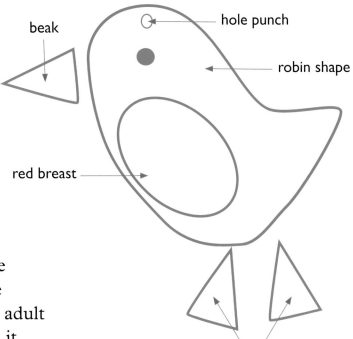

beak

hole punch

robin shape

red breast

feet

## Instructions
1. Using your pencil or crayon, draw an outline of a robin shape on the brown card and ask an adult to help you cut around it.

2. Draw a small circle on the red paper. Carefully cut it out and stick it onto the brown shape to give the robin a bright red breast.

3. Stick an eye onto the robin and punch a small hole at the top of the decoration.

4. Cut three small triangles out of the remaining brown card and stick them onto the robin: one for the beak and two for the feet.

5. Carefully thread the red ribbon or string through the hole at the top of the decoration and tie the ends of the ribbon.

# Festive Shortbread

*Ask an adult to help you bake these yummy
shortbread biscuits that have a wonderfully tangy twist.*

**Ingredients:**
125g margarine
60g caster sugar
180g plain flour
One orange

**You will need:**
A baking tray
Greaseproof paper
A wooden spoon
A large mixing bowl
A small, circular cutter
A rolling pin

## Method

1. Ask an adult to preheat the oven to 190°C (Gas Mark 5). Put the margarine and sugar into a large bowl and mix together with a wooden spoon until smooth.

2. Add the flour to the bowl. Wash and dry your hands, then knead the mixture with your hands until it turns into a smooth dough.

3. Place the dough onto a work surface that has been dusted with flour and gently roll it out until it is 1cm thick.

4. Use a circular cutter to cut circles out of the dough and place them onto a baking tray that has been lined with greaseproof paper.

5. Bake in the oven for 15 minutes, or until pale golden-brown.

6. Ask an adult to put the biscuits onto a wire rack to cool. Finely grate the zest of an orange over the top of the biscuits and sprinkle them with sugar.

# Angel Mae and the Christmas Baby

Mae Morgan lived with her mum and dad and her big brother Frankie in the flats on the corner of Trotter Street. Mae's grandma lived nearby. Soon there was going to be another person in the family, because Mae's mum was going to have a baby. It would be born around Christmas time.

Everyone was making preparations for the baby. Grandma was knitting little coats and booties. Dad was decorating the small bedroom. He painted the walls a beautiful yellow. Mum got out the old cradle that Mae and Frankie had slept in when they were babies. She put a pretty new lining in it.

"Imagine us being small enough to sleep in that!" said Frankie.

Mae tried sitting in the cradle. She could just fit if her knees were drawn up under her chin.

Mae thought about the baby a lot. She looked in her toy chest and pulled out some of her old toys. She was hoping to have some lovely new things at Christmas, so she thought she would give the baby a few of her old toys.

She didn't want to give away anything too special, like her best doll, Carol. She thought she could let the baby have her old pink rabbit and the duck who nodded his head and flapped his wings when you pulled him along. And there was the ball with the bell inside it. They were all too babyish for her now.

Carefully, Mae put the rabbit, the duck and the ball into the baby's cradle.

"What are you putting those old toys in there for?" asked Frankie. "Our new baby will be much too small to play with those." And he told Mae that at first it would be a tiny little baby, not nearly big enough to play with toys. "But he might like them when he's older," Frankie said.

"How do you know it will be a he?" Mae answered crossly. Frankie said he didn't know, but he hoped it would be so he could teach the baby to play football.

Mae slowly piled up her old toys and threw them on the floor beside her toy chest.

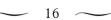

The flat where Mae and Frankie lived was on the third floor. There were a good many stairs because there wasn't a lift. Mum got tired carrying up the shopping.

Mae got tired too. She wished she could be carried like a shopping bag.

"Carry me, carry me," she moaned, drooping on the banisters at the bottom step. But Mum couldn't carry Mae and the shopping. Mae was much too old to be carried anyway.

After lunch Mum sat down for a rest. Frankie put a cushion under her poor tired feet. Mae moped about. She counted Mum's toes – one, two, three, four – up to ten. Then she started to tickle her feet. But Mum didn't want her feet tickled just then. She lay back and closed her eyes but Mae knew she wasn't really asleep.

Mae went off to find Dad. He was getting ready to clean the car. He said that Mae could help if she liked, so together they went downstairs into the street. Dad gave Mae a rag so she could polish the hubcaps. Mae rubbed away until she could see her own face. It looked a bit funny.

"Do you think our baby will be a boy or a girl?" she asked.

"Nobody knows for sure," said Dad. "But as there's you and Mum and Grandma in our family already, it would even things up if it was a boy, wouldn't it?" He ruffled Mae's hair. "You'd like to have a baby brother, wouldn't you, Mae?"

But Mae said nothing. She just went on polishing.

At school, all the children were getting ready for Christmas. Mae's teacher, Mrs Foster, helped them to make paper robins and lanterns to decorate the classroom. Then Mrs Foster told everybody that they were going to act a play about baby Jesus being born. All the Trotter Street mums and dads would be invited to watch.

Nancy Jones was going to be Mary and wear a blue hood over her long fair hair and Jim Zolinski was going to be Joseph and wear a false beard. Frankie, Harvey and Billy were going to be kings. They had gold paper crowns with jewels painted round them.

Mae wanted to be a king too, but Mrs Foster said that kings were boys' parts. Mae looked into the wooden manger for the baby Jesus. "I'll be baby Jesus, then," said Mae. She was sure she would fit into the manger if she tried very hard.

But Mrs Foster explained that they were going to wrap up a baby doll in a shawl to be baby Jesus. She said that Mae could be a cow or a sheep if she liked, but Mae certainly didn't want to be either of those. She stuck out her bottom lip and made a very cross face.

"What about being an angel?" asked Mrs Foster.

Mae didn't want to be an angel either.

"You could be the angel Gabriel," Mrs Foster told her. "That's a very special angel, a very important part."

Mae thought about this. Then she nodded her head.

"I'm going to be the angel Gave-you!" she told Frankie later.

"Angel who?" said Frankie.

"Angel Gave-you! A very special angel," said Mae proudly.

"I'm the angel Gave-you!" Mae announced, beaming, when Mum came to collect her. "Gave-you, Gave-you, Gave-you!" sang Mae as she bounced along ahead, all the way home.

"Angel Gave-you!" shouted Mae, hugging Dad round the waist when he came home from work.

"Gave me what?" asked Dad.

"Just Gave-you. That's my name in the Christmas play," Mae explained.

"Will you come and see us in it?" Frankie wanted to know.

Dad said he wasn't sure, but he would try very hard.

But when Mae and Frankie woke up on the morning of the Christmas play, neither Mum nor Dad was there! Grandma was cooking breakfast. She told them that Dad had taken Mum to the hospital in the night because the new baby was going to be born very soon.

"Will they be back in time to watch me being the angel Gave-you?" asked Mae anxiously.

"I'm afraid not," said Grandma. "But I'll be there for sure."

When Mae and Frankie arrived at school, the big hall looked very different. There was a blue curtain at one end with silver stars all over it and one big star hanging up in the middle. The smallest angels were going to stand on a row of chairs at the back. The animals were going to crouch down in front by the manger.

While the grown-ups were arriving, Mrs Foster helped the children to dress up. Mae had a white pillowcase over her front and a pair of white paper wings pinned on to the back. She was going to stand at the very end of the row because she was such a special angel.

From high up she could see all round the room. She could see all the mums and dads. Grandma was sitting in the very front row, smiling and smiling.

Then Mrs Foster sat down at the piano and all the children began to sing:

*"Away in a manger, no crib for a bed,*
*The little Lord Jesus lay down his sweet head…"*

Mary and Joseph sang, the angels sang and the animals sang. The shepherds came in and knelt down on one side of the manger. Then the three kings came in, carrying presents for baby Jesus. Mae sang very loudly.

Then she saw somebody coming in late at the very back of the room. It was Dad! He was smiling the biggest smile of all. Mae was so pleased to see him that she forgot she was in a play. She waved and shouted out, "Hello, Dad. I'm being the angel Gave-you!"

Dad put his fingers to his lips and waved back.

But Mae was waving so hard that her chair began to wobble...

and Mae wobbled too...

and then she fell right off the chair...

She hit the floor with a horrible crash, wings and all!

# Bump!

Mrs Foster stopped playing the piano. All the children stopped singing. Everyone looked at Mae. Mae held her arm where it hurt. She stuck out her bottom lip. She wanted to cry. But she didn't. Instead, she climbed up on to the chair again and went on singing:

*"The stars in the bright sky looked down where he lay,*
*The little Lord Jesus asleep in the hay…"*

Then all the people in the audience smiled and clapped a special clap for Mae for being so brave and not spoiling the play. Grandma clapped harder than anyone.

"Good old angel Gave-you!" said Dad when it was all over.

Grandma gave Frankie and Mae a hug and said it was the best Christmas play she had ever seen.

Then Dad said he had a big surprise for them. They had a new baby sister, born that morning. And Mum was going to bring her home in time for Christmas!

When Mae and Frankie went to the hospital, they looked into the cot and saw their tiny baby sister wrapped up in a white shawl. She had a funny little, crumpled up, red face and a few spikes of hair standing on end, and tiny crumpled up fingers. Mae liked the way she looked and she liked her nice baby smell. She was pleased that the baby looked so funny.

But most of all she was pleased that Mum would be home in time for Christmas.

# Pretty Paper Lanterns

*You can make lots of these pretty paper lanterns. When you've finished, ask an adult to help you hang them up.*

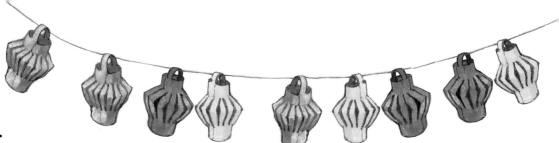

**You will need:**
Coloured A4 paper
Scissors
Sticky tape
A ruler
A pencil (or crayon)

**Instructions**

1. Using a ruler and pencil, draw two lines across the coloured paper; one along the short side and one along the long side, both about an inch from the edge.

2. Ask an adult to help you cut along the shorter line and keep the strip of paper that you cut off so that you can use it for the handle.

3. Fold the remaining paper in half so that the pencil line on the long side of the paper is visible. Cut nine slits along the folded edge right up to the pencil line.

4. Unfold the paper and gently roll it so that the shorter ends are brought together to form the lantern.

5. Stick the shorter ends together with sticky tape. Stick the strip of paper to the top of the lantern to make a handle.

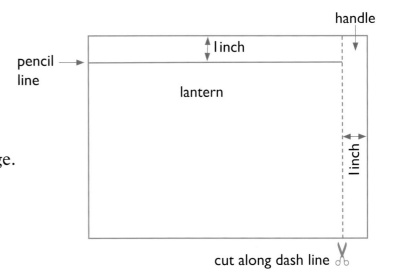

handle

pencil line → 1 inch

lantern

1 inch

cut along dash line ✂

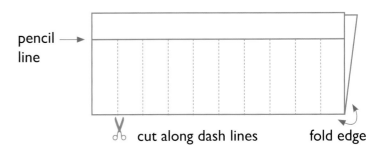

pencil line →

✂ cut along dash lines    fold edge

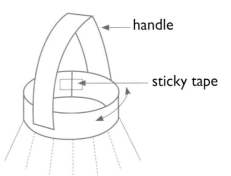

handle

sticky tape

# Ice in the Park

It's cold in the park, cold, cold,
And the wind blows sharp and keen.
The path's frosted over,
White as chalk.
Too cold to stand still,
Too cold to walk,
Better to run,
Better to shout,
Holler and wave your arms about,
See your breath come out like steam.

There's ice on the lake,
So the ducks can't swim;
Only one little hole for diving in.
It's cold in the park, cold, cold;
No more leaves on the tree.
It's almost too cold for the hungry birds,
And too cold for Olly and me.

# Snowflake Cakes

*Christmas is the best time of year for baking delicious treats for your friends and family.*

**Ingredients:**
60g margarine
60g caster sugar
60g self-raising flour
1 egg
1 tsp vanilla extract
1 tbsp milk
Icing sugar to decorate
Blue food colouring

**You will need:**
A mixing bowl
A wooden spoon
A sieve
12-hole fairycake tin
12 paper cake cases

## Method

1. Ask an adult to preheat the oven to 180°C (Gas Mark 4) and line the fairycake tin with twelve paper cases.

2. Cream the margarine and sugar together in a bowl. Add the egg and stir well.

3. Sift the flour into the bowl, then add the vanilla extract and the milk and stir until the mixture is smooth. Spoon the mixture into the paper cases until they are half full.

4. Bake in the oven for 10-12 minutes, or until golden-brown on top. Ask an adult to remove the cases from the tin and cool them on a wire rack.

5. Once the cakes are cool, sift some icing sugar into a bowl and add a drop of blue colouring. Stir in enough water to create a smooth mixture.

6. Drizzle the icing over the cakes and leave to dry. Then, sift a little bit of icing sugar over the cakes to make it look like snowflakes on a blue sky!

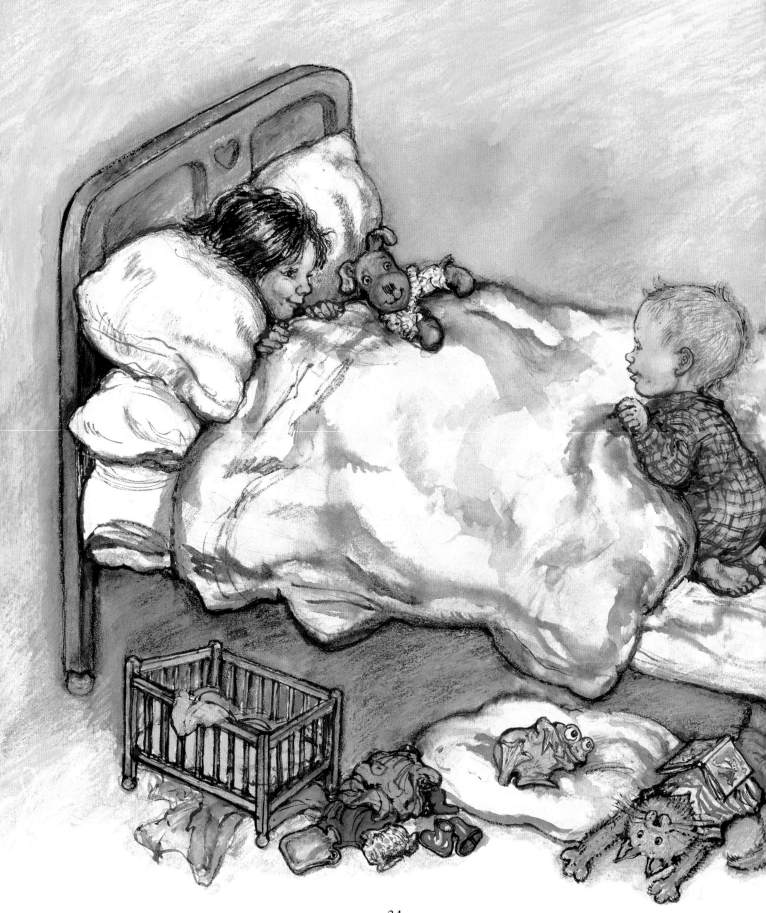

# Three in a Bed

Three in a bed
Under the cover,
Bemily, me
And Olly my brother.
He's at one end,
We're at the other,
Warm in bed
Under the cover.

# Christmas Tree Cards

*Once you've made these simple cards, write a special Christmassy message in both of them.*

**You will need:**
A4 sheet of brown card
A4 sheet of red paper
A sheet of green felt
Scissors
A glue stick
Crayons or coloured pencils

**Instructions:**
1. Fold the sheet of brown card in half to make a long thin rectangle. Ask an adult to help you cut the width of the rectangle in half, so that you are left with two folded cards.

2. Ask an adult to help you cut out a triangle from the sheet of green felt. Stick the triangle onto the centre of each card.

3. Use your crayons or coloured pencils to draw a square underneath the triangle so that it looks like a Christmas tree in a pot.

4. Draw some small circular shapes on the red paper and ask an adult to help cut them out. Stick the circles onto the tree to decorate it.

# Seasonal Tarts

*You can fill these Christmas tarts with jam or mincemeat. Dust them with a little icing sugar to make them look extra special.*

**Ingredients:**
30g caster sugar
300g plain flour
140g margarine
12 teaspoons of jam
(or mincemeat)
6 tbsp cold water

**You will need:**
A medium-sized,
circular cutter
A small, star-shaped
cutter
A mixing bowl
A rolling pin
12-hole fairycake tin

## Method

1. Ask an adult to preheat the oven to 190°C (Gas Mark 5) and to help sieve the flour into a bowl.

2. Wash and dry your hands and then rub the margarine into the flour.

3. Add the water, tablespoon by tablespoon, and knead until it becomes a moist dough. If the dough becomes too wet, add a bit more flour to the mix.

4. Roll out the pastry onto a lightly floured surface until it is 1cm thick. Cut away a third of the pastry and set it aside.

5. Grease the fairycake tin with margarine and use a round cutter to cut the pastry into twelve circles. Press the circles of pastry into the tin and scoop a teaspoon of jam into the middle of each pastry case.

6. Roll out the remaining pastry and use a star-shaped cutter to cut twelve shapes out of it. Carefully press the shapes on top of the tarts.

7. Bake in the oven for 12-15 minutes. Then ask an adult to take the tray out of the oven to cool.

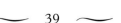

# The Snow Lady

Sam's real name was Samantha but everyone called her Sam. Sam's dog was named Micawber but everyone called him Mick. Sam and Mick were very fond of each other.

In the mornings, when Sam went to school and Sam's mum and dad and her big sister, Liz, went to work, Mick stayed at home to guard the house.

When school was over Sam walked home with her friend Barney and his dad. As soon as Mick heard Sam's footsteps he put his front paws on the windowsill and barked a joyful welcome. Sam longed to put him on his lead right away and run off up Trotter Street, with Mick pulling her along and sniffing excitedly at gates and lamp posts. But Mum was still at work and, as usual, she had arranged for Mrs Dean next door to keep an eye on Sam until everyone else came home.

Mrs Dean lived alone with her cat, Fluff. Her house was very clean and tidy. The lace curtains were snowy white and the floor was polished like a skating rink. Mrs Dean welcomed Sam with a glass of milk and two plain biscuits. Sam balanced them on her lap and tried not to drop crumbs while she and Fluff and Mrs Dean sat side by side on Mrs Dean's beautiful blue sofa and watched television.

Mick was never allowed into Mrs Dean's house. He and Fluff got on very badly whenever they met. Sam could hear him howling mournfully next door.

"Whatever has got into that dog?" said Mrs Dean.

She opened her front door and shushed at Mick from the doorstep, but he didn't take a bit of notice. He just went on howling.

Sam and Mick were both glad when they heard Mum's key in the lock.

Mrs Dean's garden was just as neat and tidy as her house. If Mick got in there and started to dig holes searching for imaginary rabbits, or picked a fight with Fluff, Mrs Dean became very cross.

Mrs Dean didn't even like Mick to be in the street. Sam and Barney and the other children often played in Trotter Street after school and Mick always joined in. But before long Mrs Dean's face would appear at her window. She would tap sharply on the pane, then put out her head and say to Sam: "That dog really ought to be chained up. My poor little Fluff is so frightened she daren't come out." Or she would say: "Would you mind asking your friends not to sit on my wall?" Or: "A little less noise, dear, please."

And that was the end of their game.

But now the weather was getting too cold to play out of doors. One night the water from a leaking drain froze on the pavement outside Sam's house, turning it into a sheet of ice. The Trotter Street children had a great time running up to it as fast as possible and seeing how far they could slide. They hung on to one another and all slid together in a chain. Wheee! It was just like the Winter Olympics! Mick ran alongside, skidding and barking.

Soon Mrs Dean popped out wearing a shawl over her shoulders.

"That's very dangerous," she said. "You might easily break your arms or legs! Do stop at once."

Everyone stopped sliding except Barney. He was at the end of the chain and just kept going. He cannoned into Harvey. Harvey cannoned into Billy, who fell against Mae, who slipped over, pulling Sam and the others with her. There was a terrific pile-up.

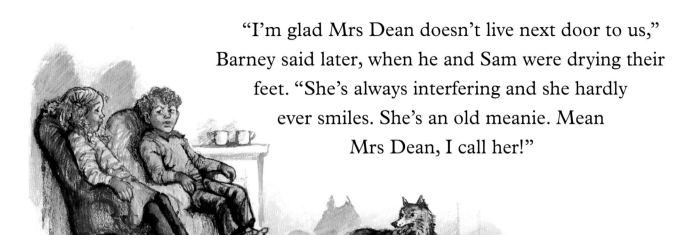

"I'm glad Mrs Dean doesn't live next door to us," Barney said later, when he and Sam were drying their feet. "She's always interfering and she hardly ever smiles. She's an old meanie. Mean Mrs Dean, I call her!"

It was getting near to Christmas. People in Trotter Street were buying Christmas trees and putting up decorations. Mrs Dean hung a wreath of plastic holly tied with red ribbons on her door.

Everyone admired it except Mick, who took a savage dislike to it. He barked fiercely every time he caught sight of it. Sam had a terrible time trying to drag him past Mrs Dean's house whenever they went for a walk.

One day Mick got out on his own and worried the ribbon until he got one end of it between his teeth. Then he pulled the whole thing down and ran off up Trotter Street with the wreath round his neck and the ribbons streaming out behind. Mrs Dean was very cross indeed. After that, Mick was in bad disgrace.

Sam was pleased when she heard Mrs Dean telling Mum that she was planning to spend Christmas with her married son. And sure enough, on the very day before Christmas Eve, Sam saw her setting out in a taxi, taking Fluff in a cat basket and a great many parcels. Hurrah! thought Sam.

Then something even better happened. Out of a slate-grey sky it began to snow. Big flakes whirled down, covering the pavements and parked cars of Trotter Street with a soft, white blanket.

Next morning the sun came out and so did Sam and Barney. They decided to build a snowman where the snow lay thickest, between Sam's front gate and Mrs Dean's. First they piled the snow into a big heap. Mick watched with interest.

Soon there was something which looked like a person with a round head, stick arms and stones for eyes, nose and mouth.

"Let's give him a top hat and a scarf and a pipe," said Barney. "Then he'll be a real snowman!"

Sam and Barney went indoors. Mum was busy but she said they could pick out some old clothes from the top of the cupboard if they liked.

But Sam and Barney could not find any of the things they wanted, only a lot of hats and dresses belonging to Mum and Liz.

"It'll just have to be a snow lady," Sam decided.

They dressed the snow lady in a hat and coat, put a shawl over her shoulders and hung a handbag on one of her stick arms. She looked very realistic.

"I know who she reminds me of," said Barney. And he moved the stones so that her mouth turned down instead of up.

He searched in the snow for some more small stones and arranged them where the snow lady's feet would have been. The words stood out clearly:

Sam giggled. The snow lady really did look rather like Mrs Dean. But Barney had not finished. He rearranged the D in Dean to make an M. Then the stones read:

"Lucky she's away," said Sam. "How awful it would be if she could see it!" Then they heard Mum calling and ran indoors taking Mick with them.

The rest of the day was so busy and exciting that Sam and Barney forgot all about the snow lady.

Late that night, long after Barney had wished them all a Happy Christmas and gone home to hang up his stocking, Sam was too excited to sleep. She got up, drew the curtains back a little and looked out at the street. Everything looked white and Christmassy, but big black clouds were scudding across the moon. When she caught sight of the snow lady, still standing there all alone, it gave her quite a shock.

Then Sam saw a taxi draw up. Out stepped Mrs Dean! The driver unloaded Fluff and the luggage and helped her into the house. Mrs Dean walked right past the snow lady without even glancing at her.

But she'll see her tomorrow when it's light, thought Sam. It will hurt her feelings. And on Christmas Day too!

Sam decided she must go out at once and kick away the stones which spelled out the snow lady's name. She would take off the clothes too.

It was *terribly important!*

Sam crept quietly downstairs and began to put on her coat over her pyjamas. But Mick heard her and came running, barking and making a great fuss.

Mum put her head round the living room door. "Whatever are you doing, Sam? You can't go out at this time of night!" And she packed Sam firmly off upstairs. "The sooner you're asleep the sooner Christmas will be here," she said, kissing her goodnight.

Still Sam could not get to sleep. She felt too awful about Mrs Dean. When she did fall asleep her dreams were full of excited visions of Mick, Fluff and the snow lady and lots of Christmas parcels all tied up with yards and yards of red ribbon. Mrs Dean was inside one of the parcels. She jumped out and then they were all running and running… But it was not feet which Sam heard in her sleep. It was rain.

When Sam woke
up it was still dark.
Christmas morning!
And yes, the stocking at
the foot of her bed was
full of exciting surprises.
But Sam did not put
on her light yet.

Instead she ran to
the window. She could hardly see out because rivulets of water were
streaming down the pane. Below, in the street, Sam could just see the snow
lady. She seemed to have slumped back against the gate post and all around
her lay a puddle of water.

Then a great, warm hope leapt up inside Sam. She skipped back into bed
and began to open her stocking.

As soon as Christmas Day had begun properly and all the family
had kissed each other and given their presents, Sam slipped
out of the front door.

It had stopped raining. The snow lady had
collapsed altogether. Her hat had fallen
over her face and her clothes were limp
and dripping.

She kicked the stones and scattered
them about. Then she picked
up the snow lady's clothes and
pushed them into the dustbin.

She was only just in time. Mrs Dean's front door opened and out came Mrs Dean, dressed for church.

Mum hurried to their doorstep to call out "Merry Christmas, Mrs Dean! I didn't know you'd come back!"

"A merry Christmas to you all, Mrs Robinson. My son and his wife have flu and couldn't have me to stay after all," said Mrs Dean.

"Then of course you must come and have Christmas dinner with us," Mum said at once.

"Why, thank you! That's very kind," said Mrs Dean. And her face melted.

Sam stood right in front of what was left of the snow lady.
The name which had stood out so clearly in the snow was now just
a jumble of stones lying in a pool of water. Sam shuffled them about
with her feet, just in case.

"I expect you wish the snow had lasted longer," Mrs Dean
said to Sam.

"Oh no, I don't mind a bit, really," said Sam. And she gave
Mrs Dean one of her biggest most Christmassy smiles.

# Gingerbread Snowmen

*Ask an adult to help you bake these crisp and crunchy gingerbread snowmen.*

**Ingredients:**
125g margarine
175g light soft brown sugar
350g plain flour
1 tsp bicarbonate of soda
2 tsp ground ginger
1 tsp ground cinnamon
4 tbsp golden syrup
1 egg

**You will need:**
A snowman-shaped cutter
Two large baking trays
Greaseproof paper
Clingfilm
A sieve
A wooden spoon
A large mixing bowl
A rolling pin

**Method**

1. Ask an adult to preheat the oven to 180°C (Gas Mark 4) and put the dry ingredients into a large bowl. Add the margarine, wash and dry your hands, then rub the margarine into the mixture until it looks like breadcrumbs.

2. Lightly beat the egg and golden syrup together in a separate bowl then add to the large bowl, mixing until everything sticks together.

3. Tip the dough out onto a lightly floured surface and knead briefly until smooth. Wrap the dough in clingfilm and leave to chill in the fridge for 15 minutes.

4. Line two baking trays with greaseproof paper. Roll the dough out until it is 1cm thick. Cut out snowman shapes with your cutter and place them on the baking tray, leaving a gap between them.

5. Bake for 12-15 minutes, or until lightly golden-brown. When they're ready, ask an adult to take the trays out of the oven to cool.

6. When the biscuits have cooled, dust them with icing sugar, or tip some icing sugar into a bowl, mix with a little water to make a paste and then drizzle the icing onto your biscuits.

# Christmas Crackers

*You can make your very own Christmas crackers
to brighten up any festive table.*

**You will need:**
Toilet roll tube
Tissue Paper
A4 coloured paper
Pencil (or crayon)
Ribbon (or string)
Sticky tape
A chocolate coin (or small gift)

**Instructions:**

1. On a small piece of paper, use a pencil to write a joke and the answer to the joke.

2. To make a party hat, fold the coloured paper in half so that it looks like a long rectangle. Ask an adult to help draw five triangle shapes, each about 5cm tall, along the fold line of the paper. Cut out the triangles so that you are left with two pieces of paper.

3. Put the two pieces of paper next to each other and join them in the middle with sticky tape. Join the two ends together with sticky tape to complete the crown.

4. Put the chocolate coin, paper crown and the homemade joke card in the toilet roll tube.

5. Place the tube onto the tissue paper, leaving a few inches of paper either side of it. Roll the tissue paper around the tube until you come to the end. Add a piece of tape to secure the tissue paper in place.

6. Gently twist the tissue paper at each end of the tube and tie off each end of the cracker with ribbon.

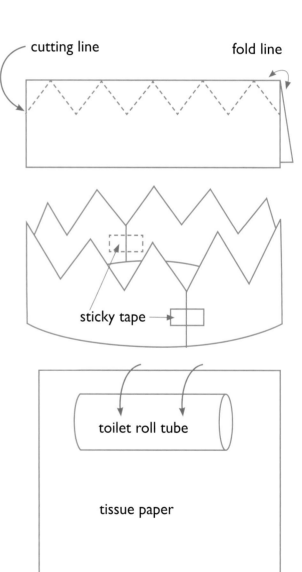

cutting line          fold line

sticky tape →

toilet roll tube

tissue paper

# Hoping

Grey day,
Dark colour,
Hurry home,
Shut the door.
Think of a time
When there will be
Decorations
On a tree.
Tangarines
And hot mince pies,
A bulging stocking,
A Christmas surprise!

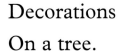

# ABOUT THE AUTHOR

Shirley Hughes has illustrated more than
200 children's books and is one of the
best-loved writers for children.
She has won the Kate Greenaway Medal
twice and has been awarded an OBE for her
distinguished service to children's literature.
In 2007, *Dogger* was voted the UK's
favourite Kate Greenaway Medal-winning
book of all time.